For my little cubs, Lyra and Emi.

First published in 2023 in Great Britain by Rocket Bird Books
an imprint of Barrington Stoke Ltd
18 Walker Street, Edinburgh, EH3 7LP

www.rocketbirdbooks.co.uk

Copyright © 2023 Owen Davey

The moral right of Owen Davey to be identified as the author and illustrator of this work has been asserted in accordance with the Copyright, Designs and Patents Act, 1988.

All rights reserved.

A CIP catalogue record for this book is available from the British Library upon request.

ISBN: 978-1-91539-500-9
Printed in China
1 3 5 7 9 10 8 6 4 2

MIX
Paper from responsible sources
FSC® C104723

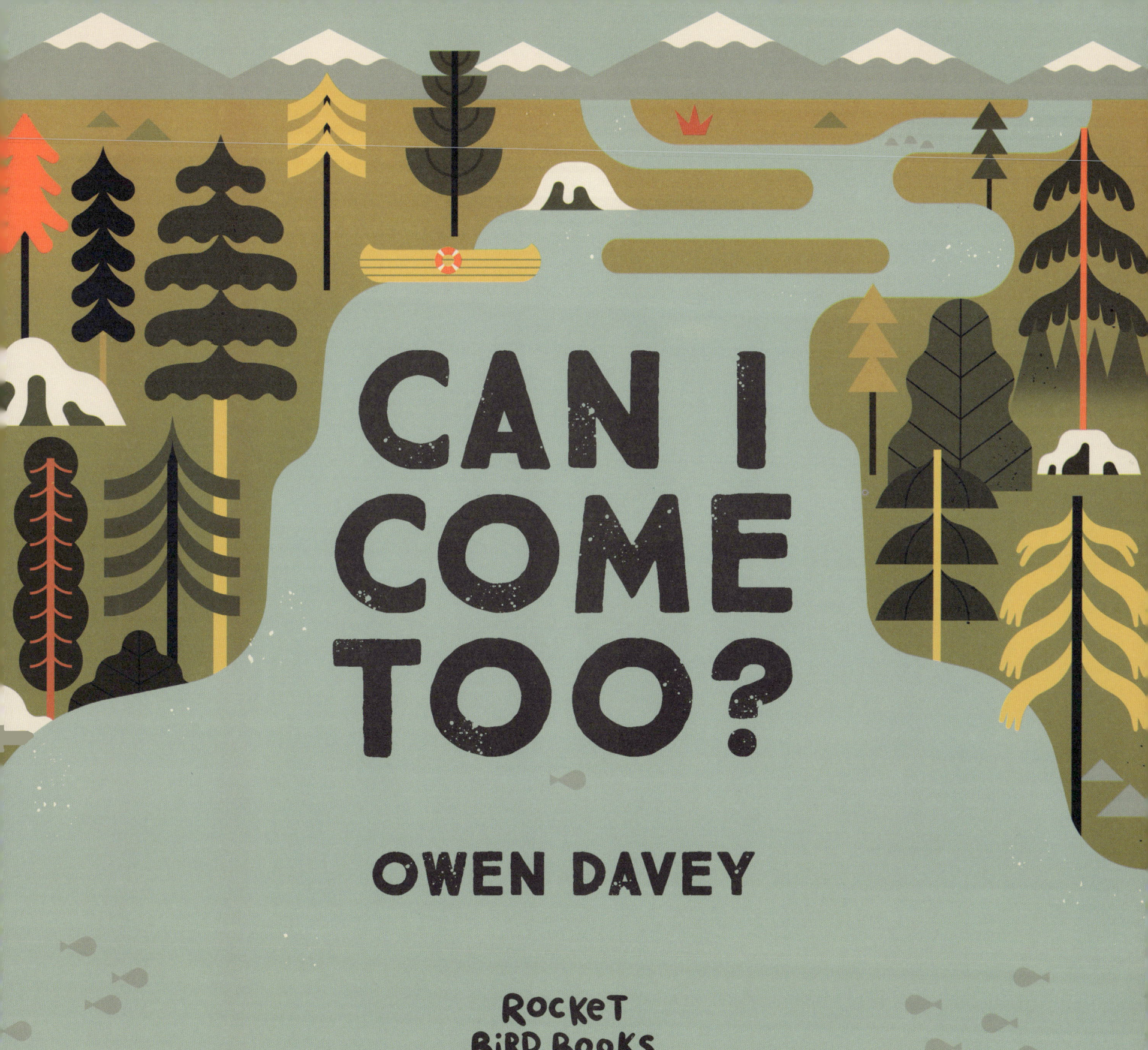

Today, Teddy is off to the spot where the river meets the sea.
"Can I come too?" asks Cub, running to catch up.

They haven't even left the garden when Cub falls over. Oh dear.
"Keep an eye on Cub!" Dad calls to Teddy.

"What are we going to play?" asks Cub.

"We're not playing," says Teddy. "I'm busy today.
I want to catch a fish and I can't have silly cubs getting in my way."

It feels a little lonely as Teddy rows away.
"Teddy, wait for me!" shouts Cub.

Cub skips along the rocks, chasing after Teddy's canoe.
"Can I come too?"

But a crab scuttles across Cub's path and . . .

Oh what a shame,
they've lost the oar.
They can't use the canoe now.
Teddy will have to fish
from the riverbank.

"Can I have a go?" asks Cub.

"No," says Teddy. "This is MY fishing rod.
Little paws will just get it tangled. Wait over there."

What a lovely fishing rod.
Cub runs to show Teddy.

"Look what I made, Teddy! Look what I made!"

But Cub hasn't spotted Teddy's fishing tin on the ground.

Oh dear, now both rods are broken.

Teddy will have to use the fishing net instead.
"I'll carry it for you," says Cub.

"Fine. But don't drop it," says Teddy.

"What about that one?" asks Cub.

It seems Teddy needs some space. "Go and wait over there," growls Teddy. "Little cubs only get in the way."

Cub sits down to watch the river rush by. "All this fishing is very tiring," thinks Cub with a great big YAWN.

For a moment, Teddy doesn't know what to say.

"I'm sorry, Cub. I'm sorry I said little cubs get in the way. I was wrong."

"That's okay," said Cub. "But what do we do now?
Do we keep it as a pet?"

"We . . . Well . . . we can do whatever you want, Cub," says Teddy.
"What do you think is best?"

"I'm going fishing again tomorrow," says Cub.

"Can I come too?" asks Teddy.